STAR WARS ADVENTURES

2

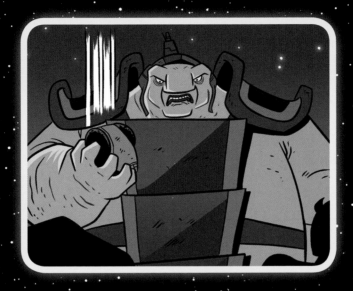

BETTER THE DEVIL YOU KNOW, PART 2

Writer: Cavan Scott
Artist: Derek Charm
Letterer: Tom B. Long

TALES FROM WILD SPACE "THE FLAT MOUNTAIN OF YAVIN"

SEE PAGE 17

Writers: Elsa Charretier & Pierrick Colinet
Artist: Elsa Charretier
Colorist: Sarah Stern
Letterer: Tom B. Long

ABDO Spotlight · IDW · Disney · Lucasfilm

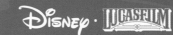

ABDOBOOKS.COM

Reinforced library bound edition published in 2019 by Spotlight, a division of ABDO,
PO Box 398166, Minneapolis, Minnesota 55439. Spotlight produces high-quality
reinforced library bound editions for schools and libraries.
Published by agreement with IDW.

Printed in the United States of America, North Mankato, Minnesota.
092018
012019

THIS BOOK CONTAINS
RECYCLED MATERIALS

Library of Congress Control Number: 2018945152

Publisher's Cataloging-in-Publication Data

Names: Scott, Cavan; Charretier, Elsa; Colinet, Pierrick, authors. | Charm, Derek; Charretier,
    Elsa; Stern, Sarah, illustrators.
Title: Star Wars adventures #2: better the devil you know, part 2 / by Cavan Scott, Elsa
    Charretier, and Pierrick Colinet ; illustrated by Derek Charm, Elsa Charretier and Sarah
    Stern.
Description: Minneapolis, Minnesota : Spotlight, 2019. | Series: Star Wars adventures
Summary: Rey has to outwit the off-worlders that captured Unkar Plutt, and Lieutenant
    Evaan Verlaine leads a dangerous mission to infiltrate an Imperial Star Destroyer.
Identifiers: ISBN 9781532142864 (lib. bdg.)
Subjects: LCSH: Star Wars fiction--Juvenile fiction. | Space warfare--Juvenile fiction. |
    Extraterrestrial beings--Juvenile fiction. | Good and evil--Juvenile fiction. | Heroes--
    Juvenile fiction.
Classification: DDC 741.5--dc23

Spotlight

A Division of ABDO
abdobooks.com

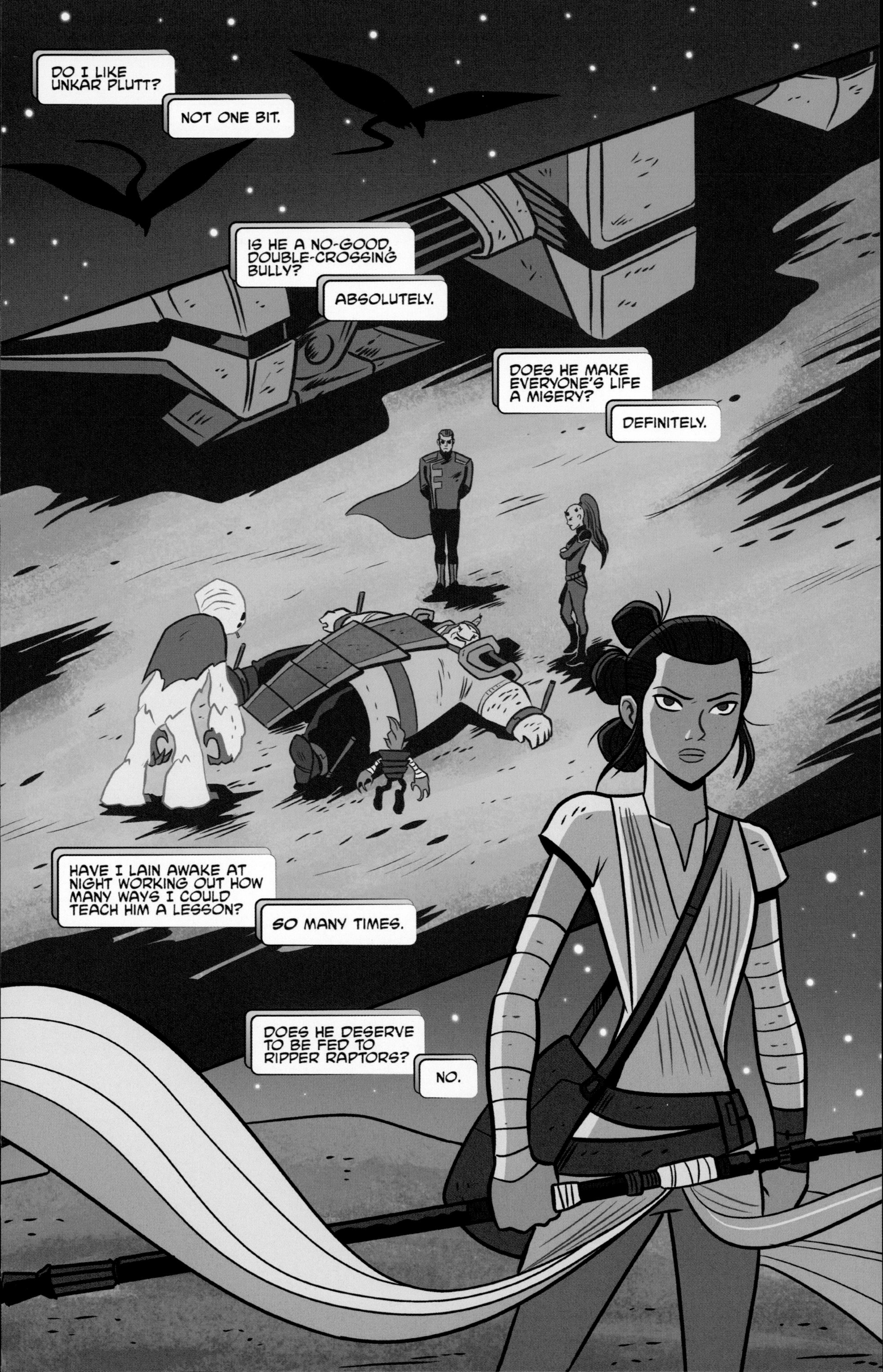
DO I LIKE UNKAR PLUTT?
NOT ONE BIT.
IS HE A NO-GOOD, DOUBLE-CROSSING BULLY?
ABSOLUTELY.
DOES HE MAKE EVERYONE'S LIFE A MISERY?
DEFINITELY.
HAVE I LAIN AWAKE AT NIGHT WORKING OUT HOW MANY WAYS I COULD TEACH HIM A LESSON?
SO MANY TIMES.
DOES HE DESERVE TO BE FED TO RIPPER RAPTORS?
NO.

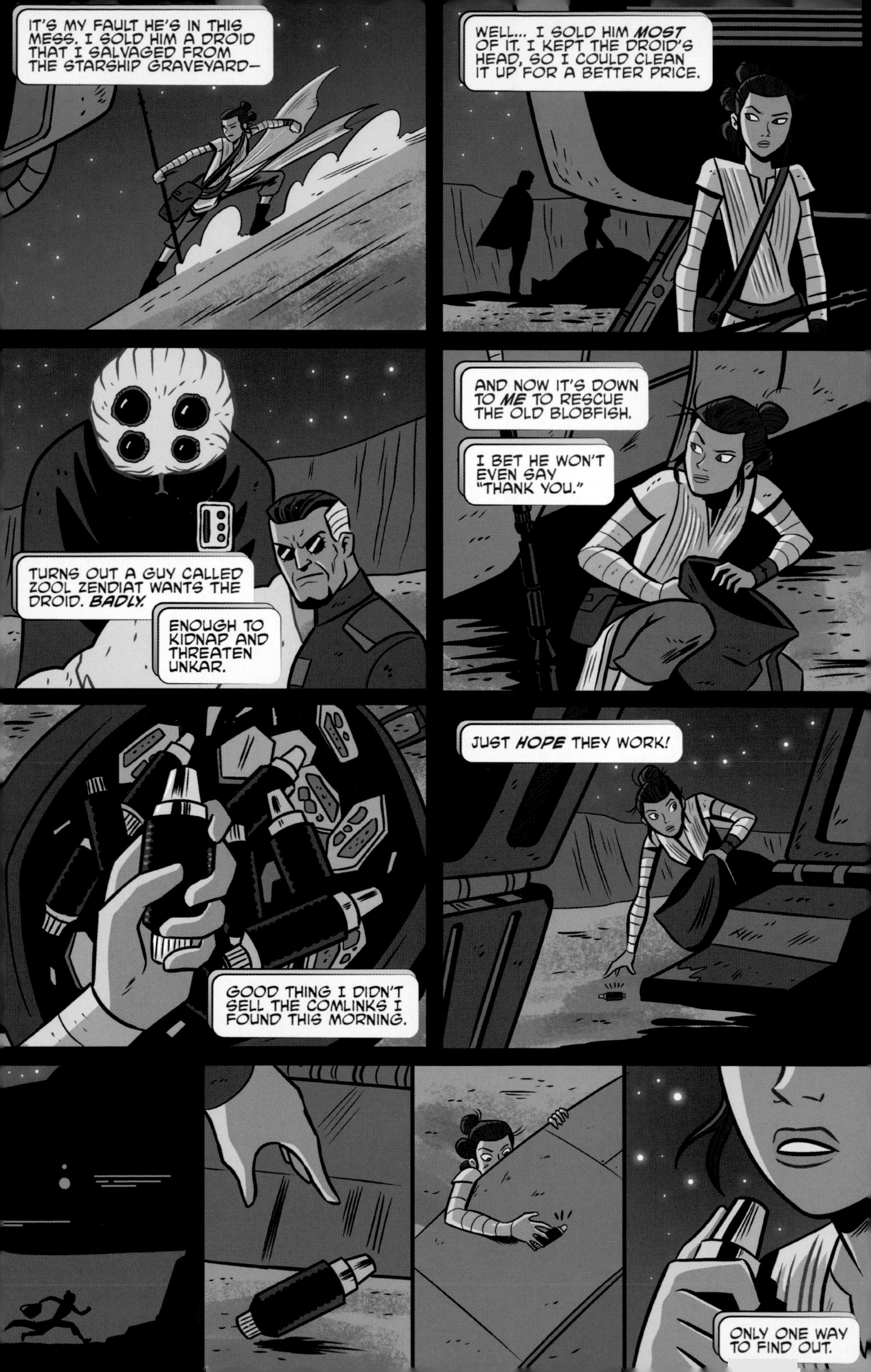
IT'S MY FAULT HE'S IN THIS MESS. I SOLD HIM A DROID THAT I SALVAGED FROM THE STARSHIP GRAVEYARD—
WELL... I SOLD HIM *MOST* OF IT. I KEPT THE DROID'S HEAD, SO I COULD CLEAN IT UP FOR A BETTER PRICE.
TURNS OUT A GUY CALLED ZOOL ZENDIAT WANTS THE DROID. *BADLY.*
ENOUGH TO KIDNAP AND THREATEN UNKAR.
AND NOW IT'S DOWN TO *ME* TO RESCUE THE OLD BLOBFISH.
I BET HE WON'T EVEN SAY "THANK YOU."
GOOD THING I DIDN'T SELL THE COMLINKS I FOUND THIS MORNING.
JUST *HOPE* THEY WORK!
ONLY ONE WAY TO FIND OUT.

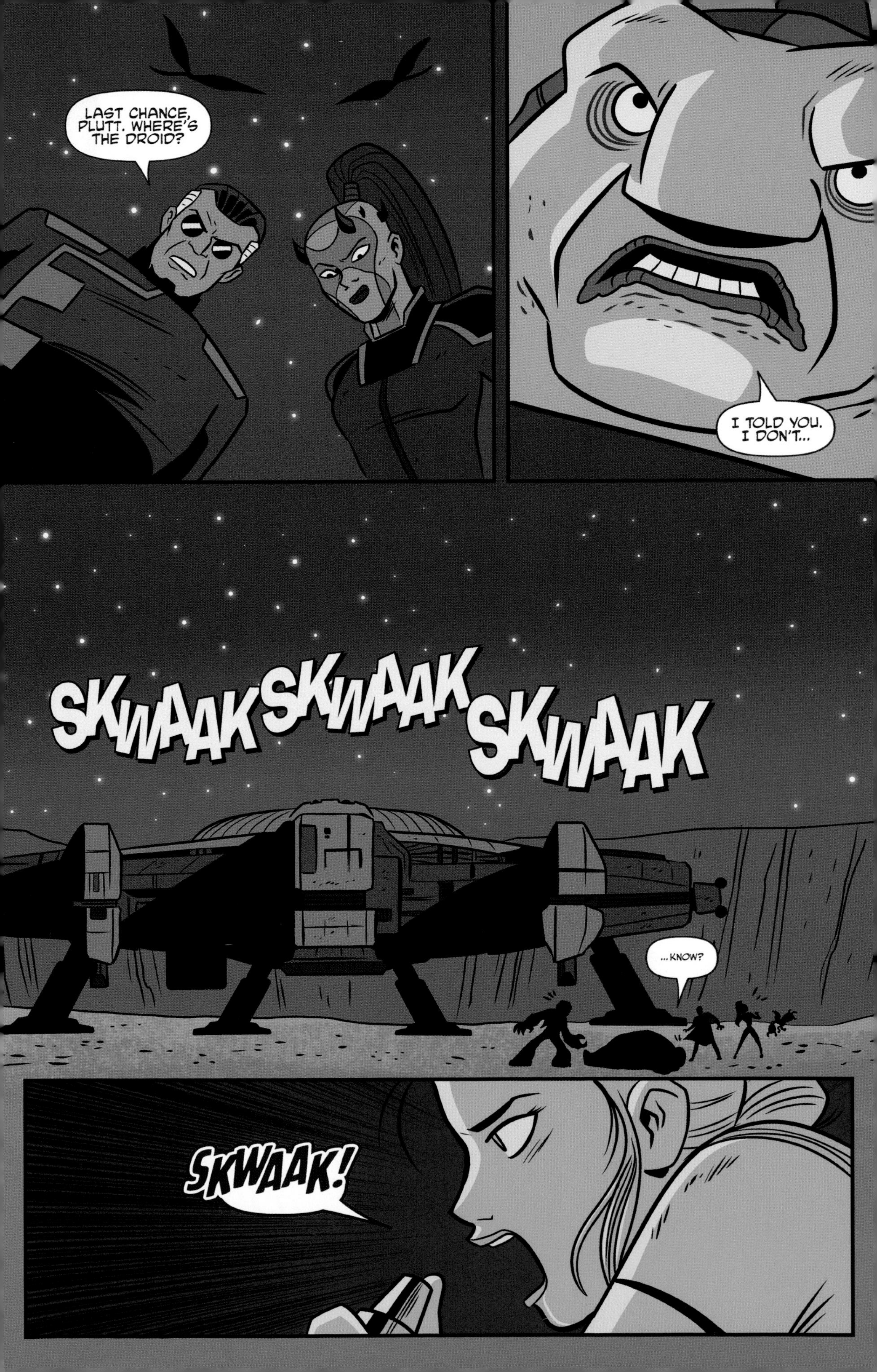
LAST CHANCE, PLUTT. WHERE'S THE DROID?
I TOLD YOU. I DON'T...
SKWAAK SKWAAK SKWAAK
...KNOW?
SKWAAK!

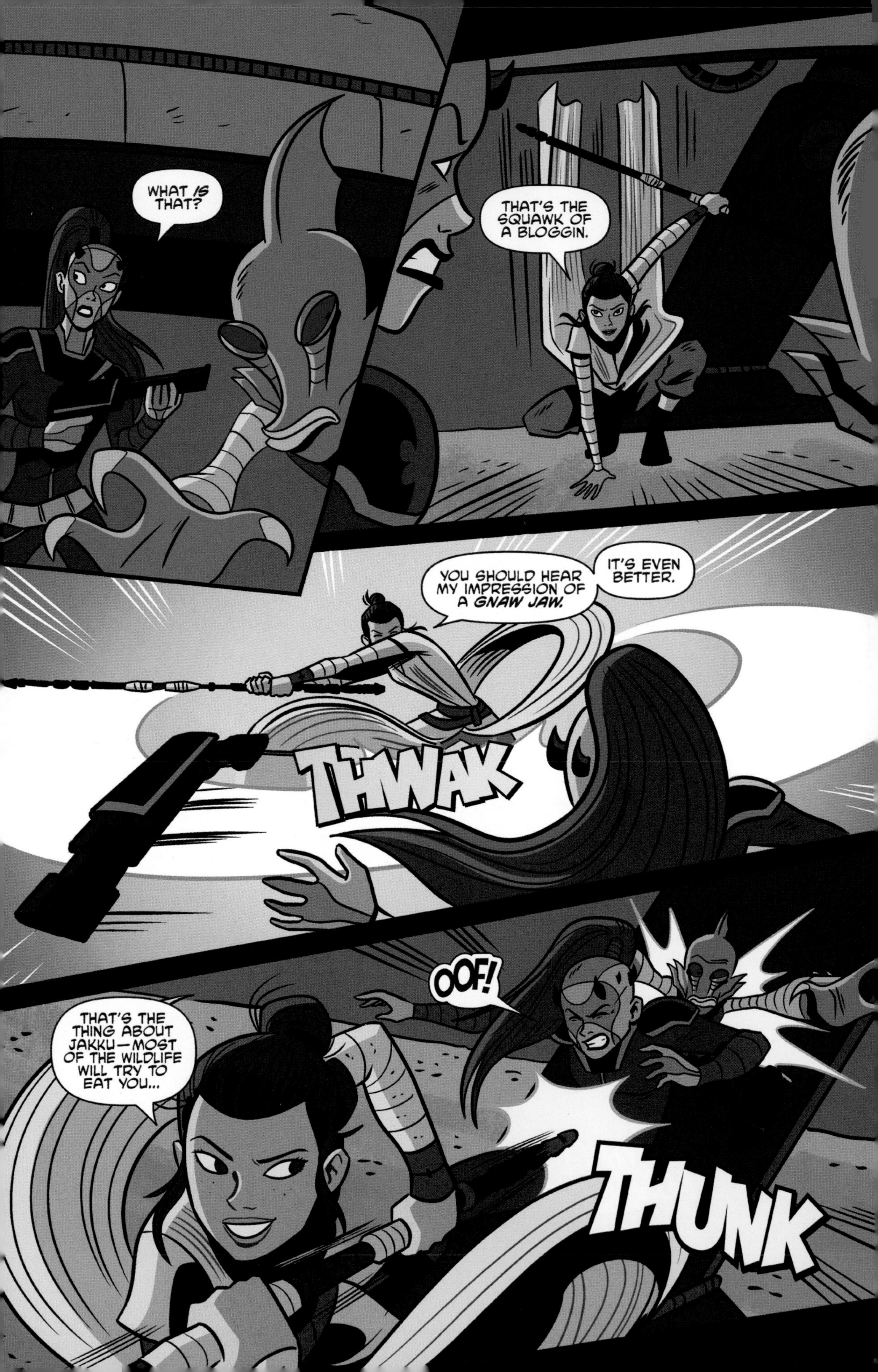
WHAT IS THAT?
THAT'S THE SQUAWK OF A BLOGGIN.
YOU SHOULD HEAR MY IMPRESSION OF A GNAW JAW.
IT'S EVEN BETTER.
THWAK
THAT'S THE THING ABOUT JAKKU—MOST OF THE WILDLIFE WILL TRY TO EAT YOU...
OOF!
THUNK

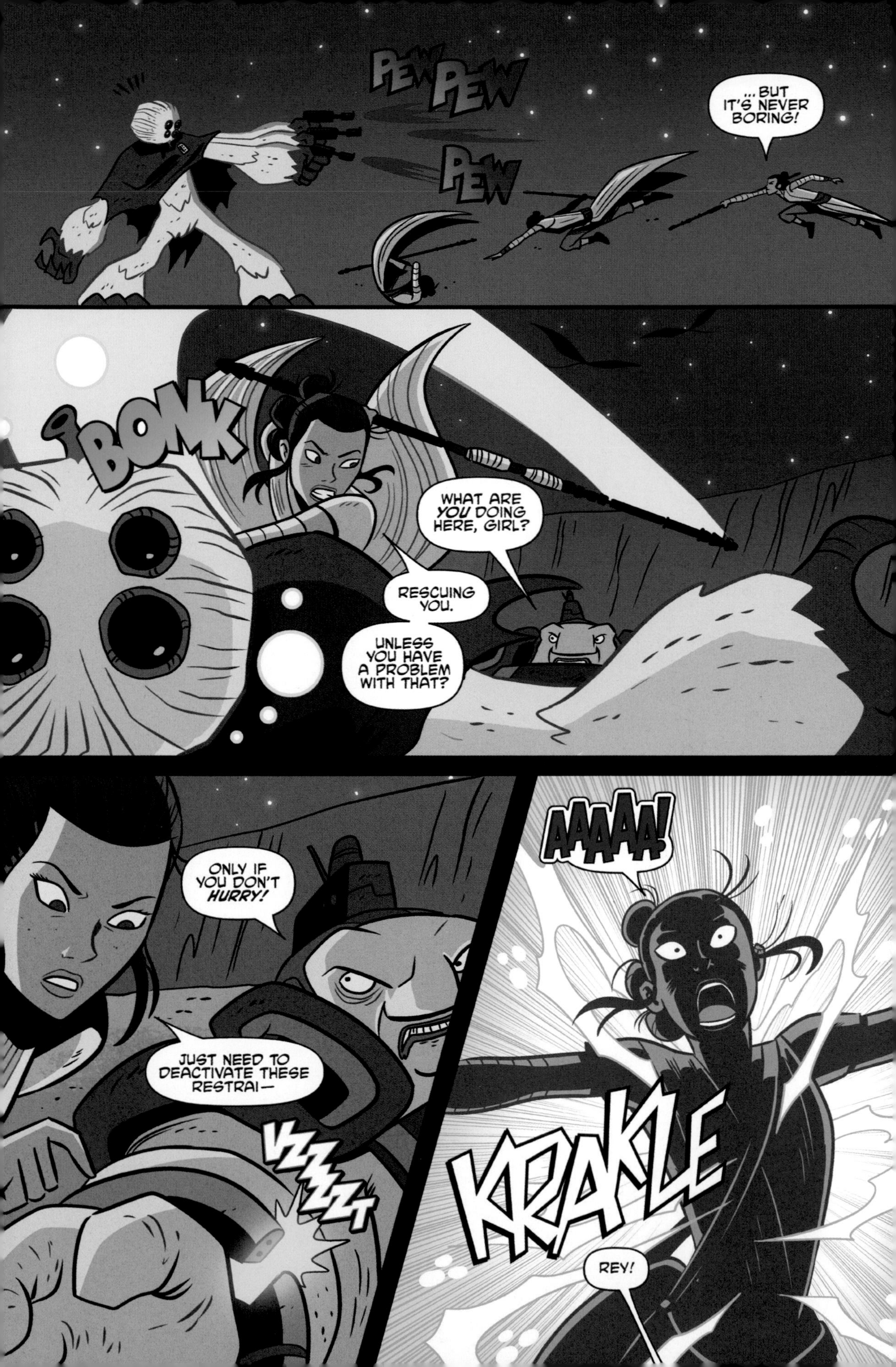
PEW PEW
PEW
...BUT IT'S NEVER BORING!
BONK
WHAT ARE YOU DOING HERE, GIRL?
RESCUING YOU.
UNLESS YOU HAVE A PROBLEM WITH THAT?
ONLY IF YOU DON'T HURRY!
JUST NEED TO DEACTIVATE THESE RESTRAI—
VZZZZT
AAAAA!
KRAKLE
REY!

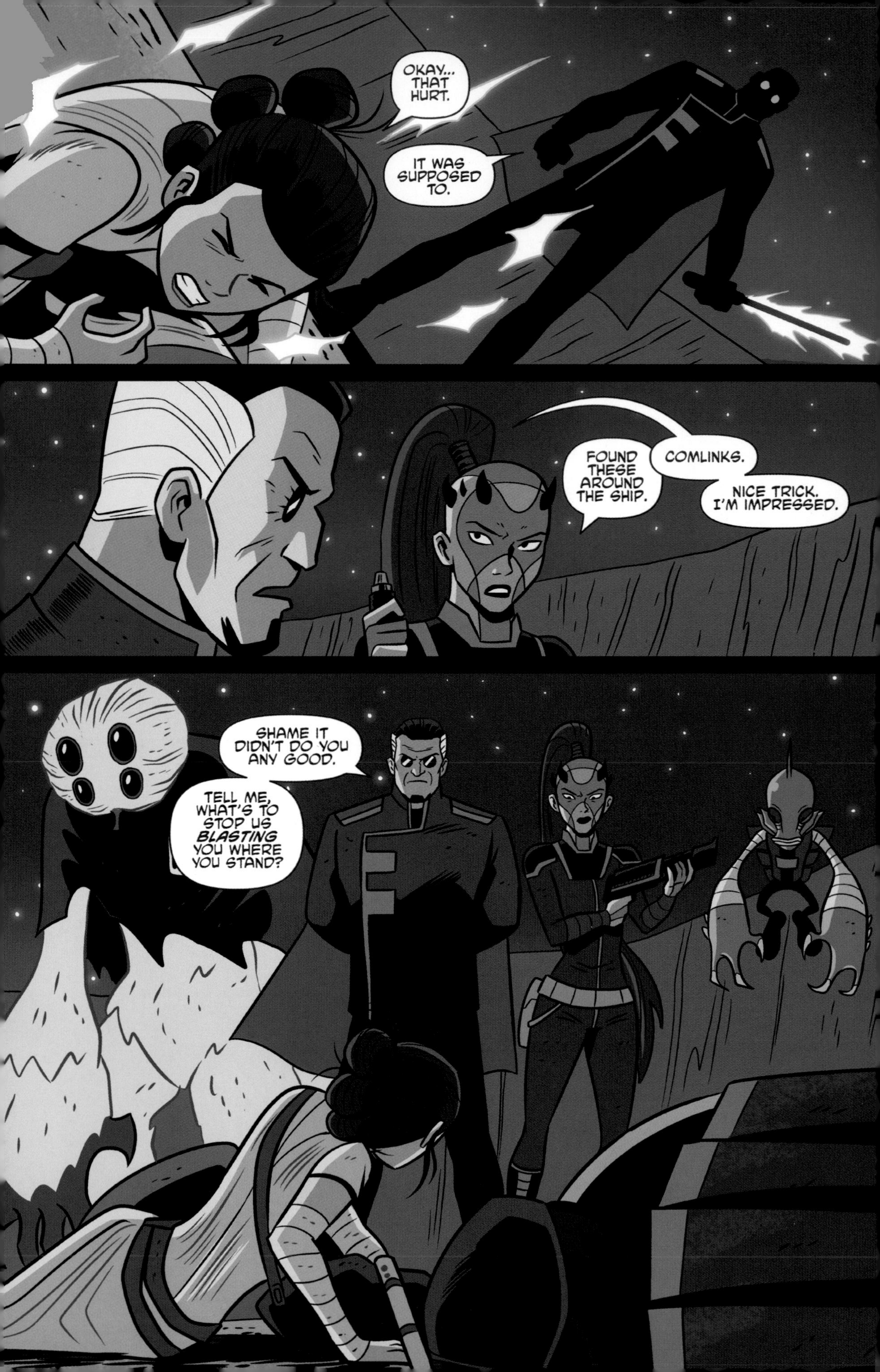
OKAY... THAT HURT.
IT WAS SUPPOSED TO.
FOUND THESE AROUND THE SHIP.
COMLINKS.
NICE TRICK. I'M IMPRESSED.
SHAME IT DIDN'T DO YOU ANY GOOD.
TELL ME, WHAT'S TO STOP US *BLASTING* YOU WHERE YOU STAND?

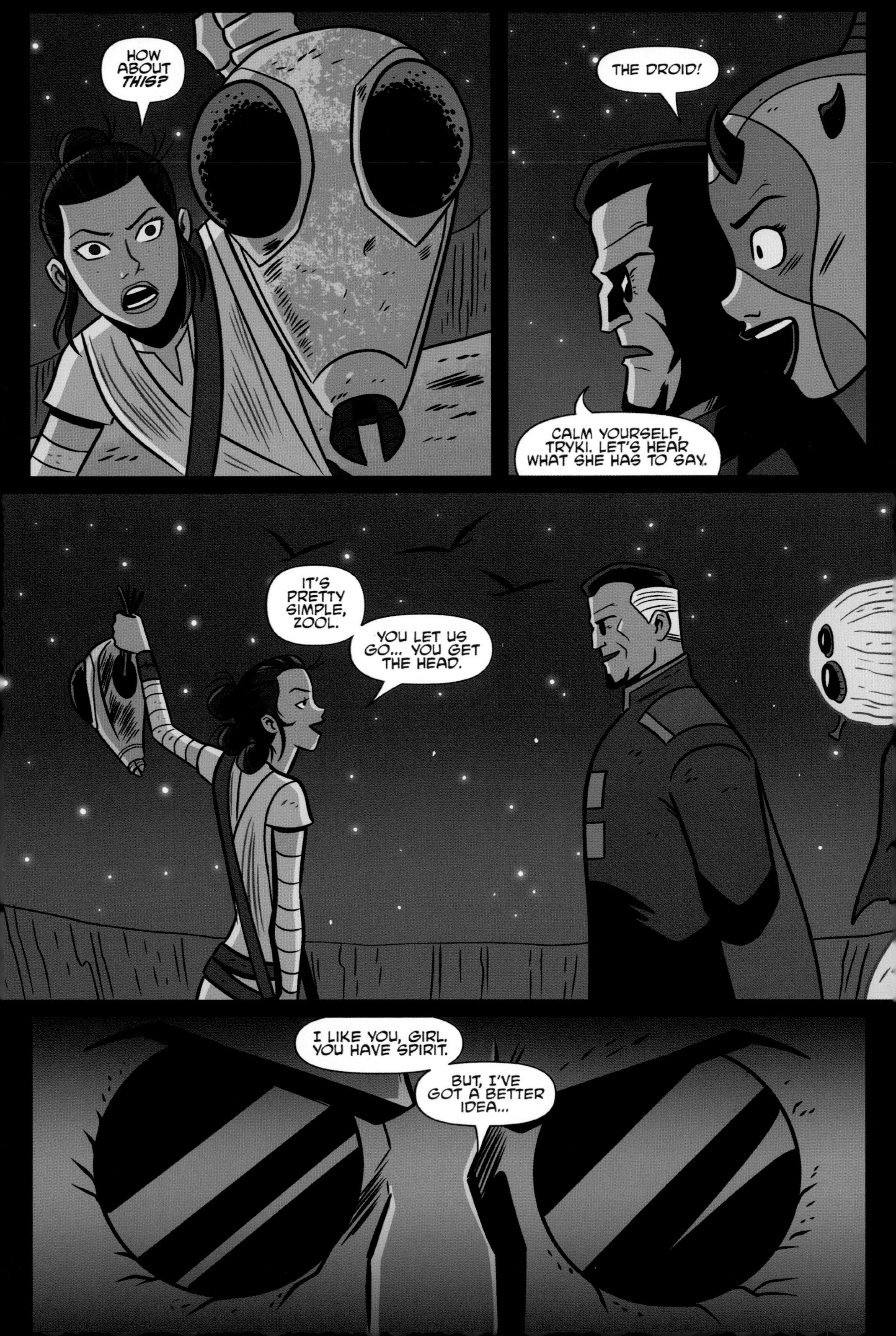
HOW ABOUT *THIS?*
THE DROID!
CALM YOURSELF, TRYKI. LET'S HEAR WHAT SHE HAS TO SAY.
IT'S PRETTY SIMPLE, ZOOL.
YOU LET US GO... YOU GET THE HEAD.
I LIKE YOU, GIRL. YOU HAVE SPIRIT.
BUT, I'VE GOT A BETTER IDEA...

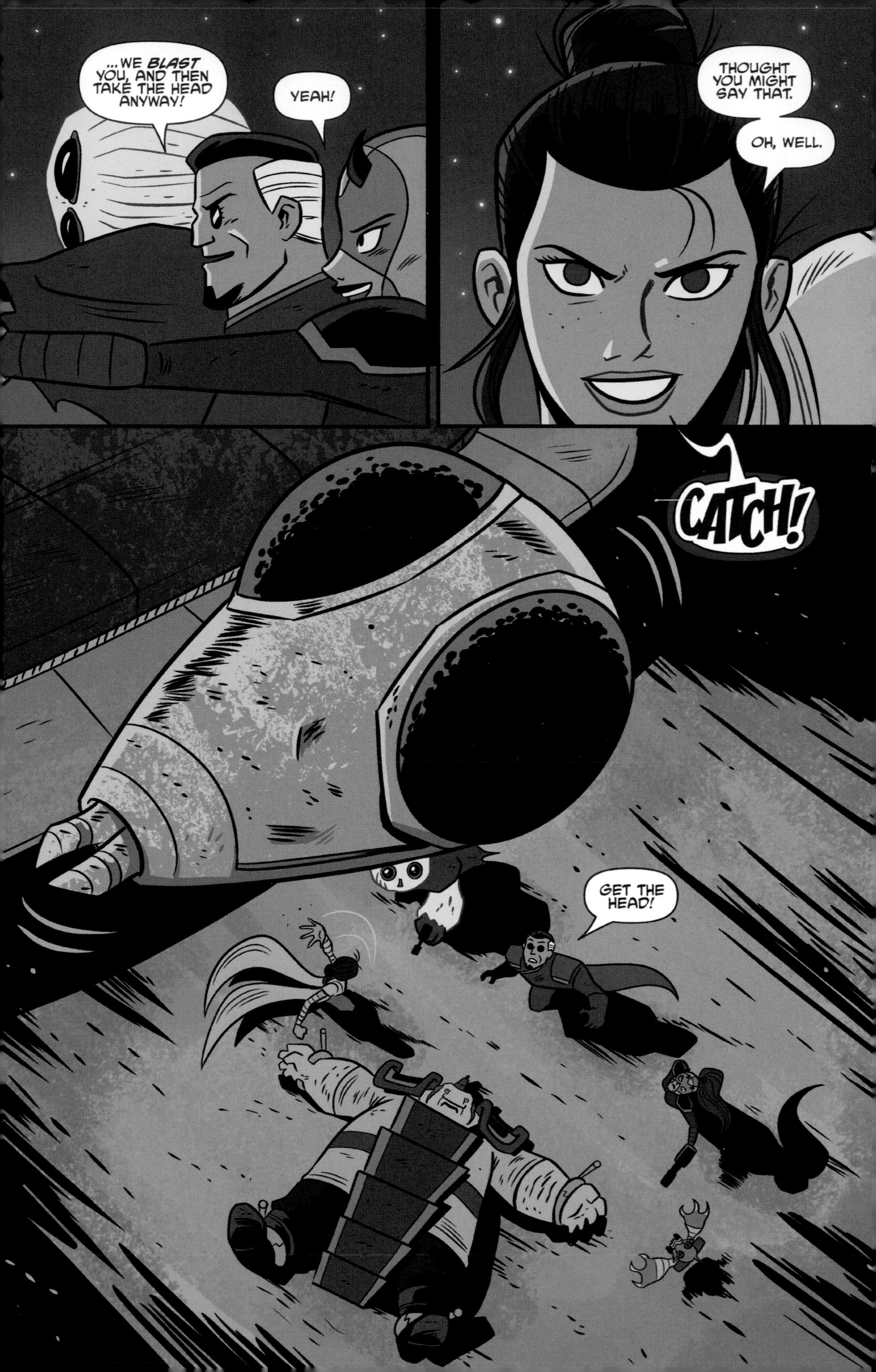
...WE BLAST YOU, AND THEN TAKE THE HEAD ANYWAY!
YEAH!
THOUGHT YOU MIGHT SAY THAT.
OH, WELL.
CATCH!
GET THE HEAD!

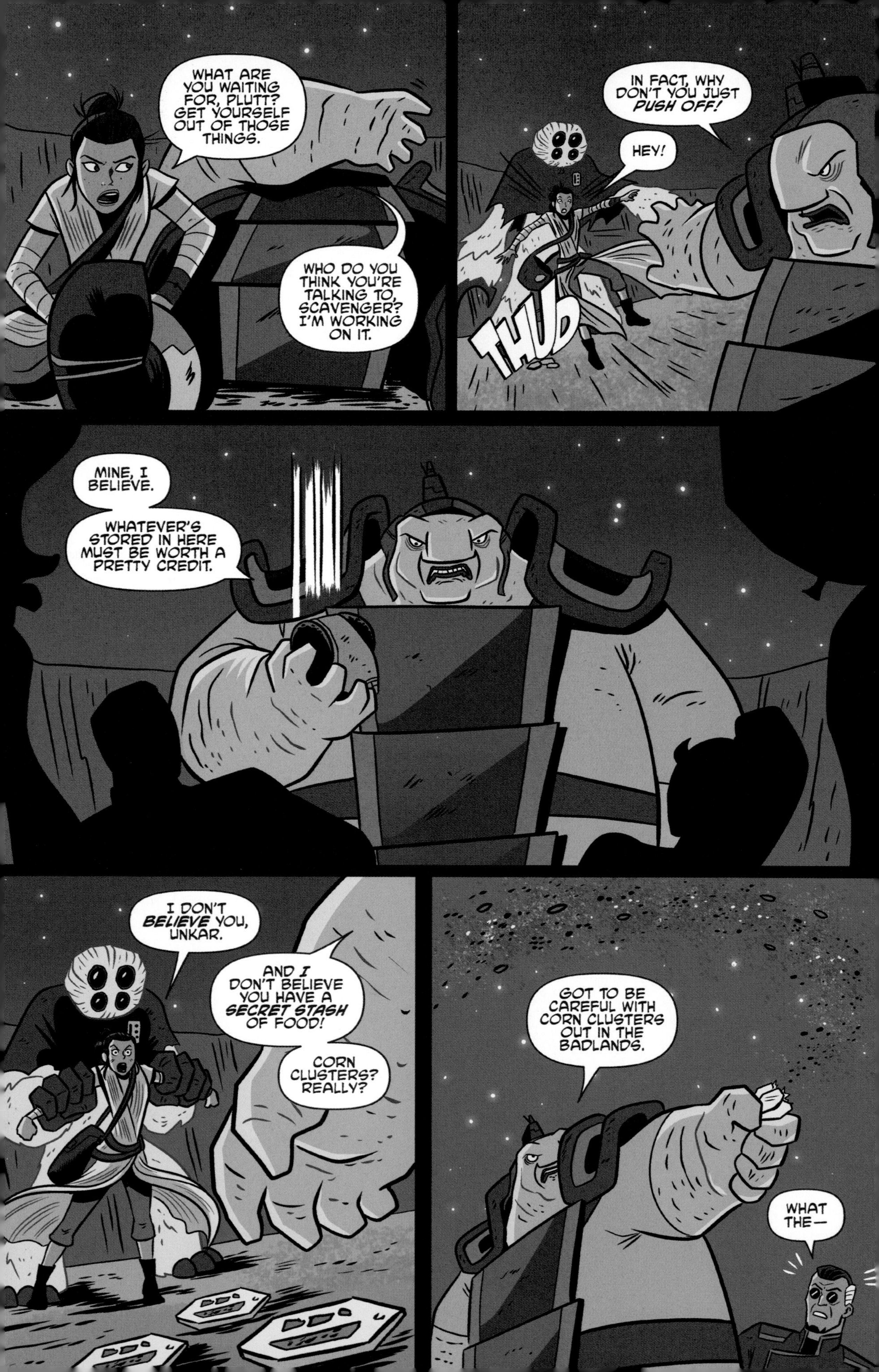
WHAT ARE YOU WAITING FOR, PLUTT? GET YOURSELF OUT OF THOSE THINGS.
WHO DO YOU THINK YOU'RE TALKING TO, SCAVENGER? I'M WORKING ON IT.
IN FACT, WHY DON'T YOU JUST PUSH OFF!
HEY!
THUD
MINE, I BELIEVE.
WHATEVER'S STORED IN HERE MUST BE WORTH A PRETTY CREDIT.
I DON'T BELIEVE YOU, UNKAR.
AND I DON'T BELIEVE YOU HAVE A SECRET STASH OF FOOD!
CORN CLUSTERS? REALLY?
GOT TO BE CAREFUL WITH CORN CLUSTERS OUT IN THE BADLANDS.
WHAT THE—

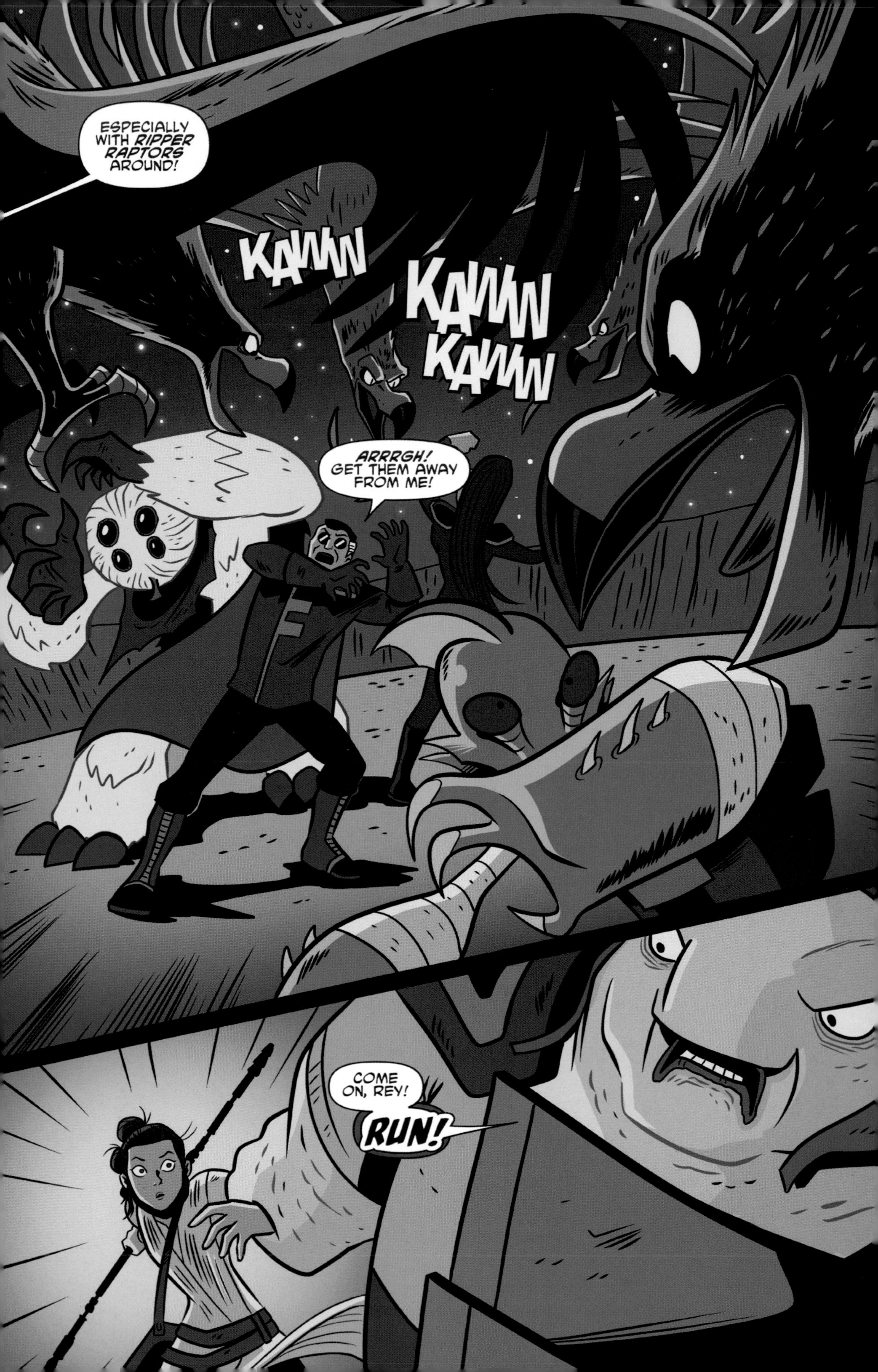
ESPECIALLY WITH RIPPER RAPTORS AROUND!
KAWW
KAWW KAWW
ARRRGH! GET THEM AWAY FROM ME!
COME ON, REY!
RUN!

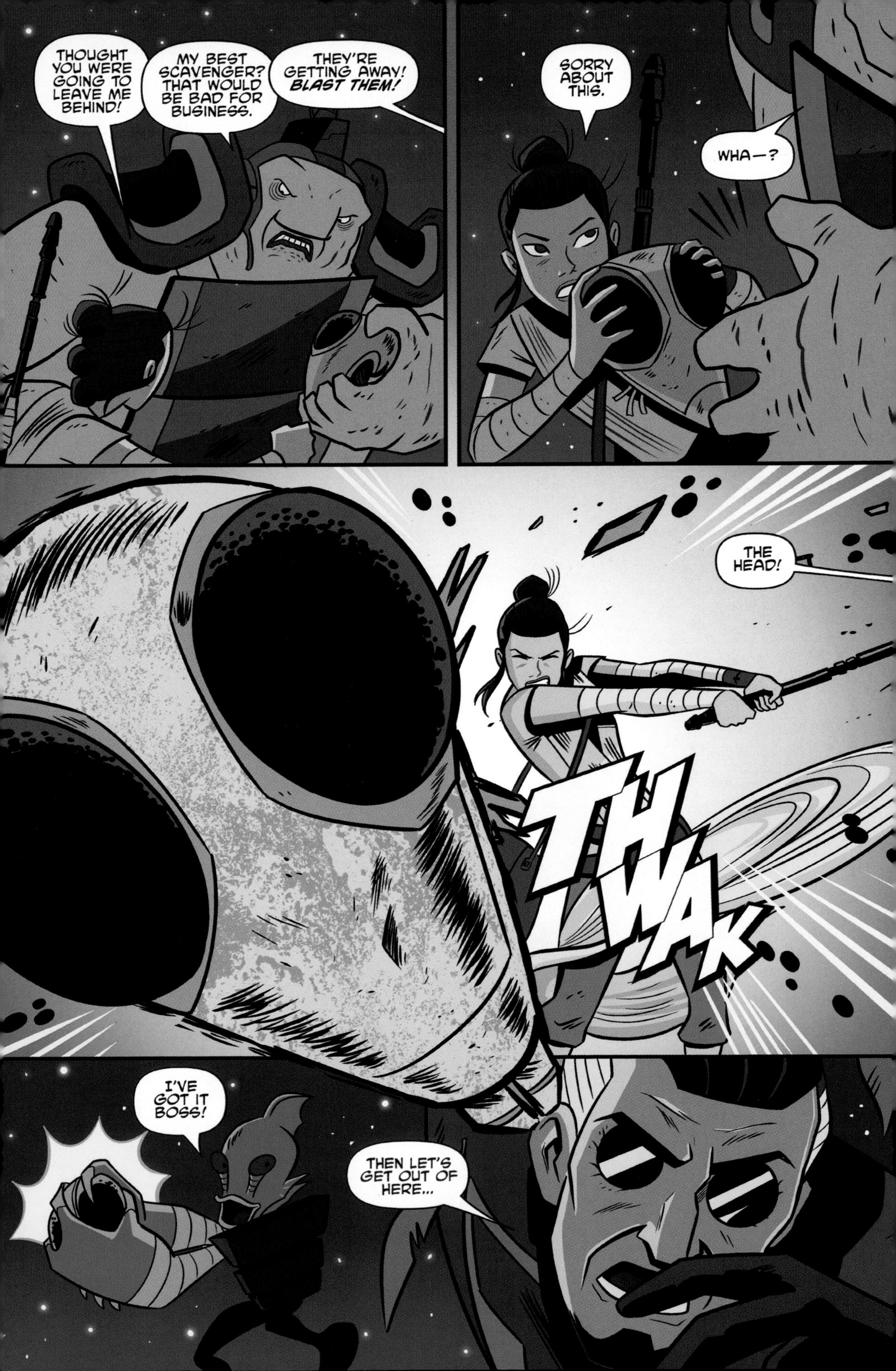
THOUGHT YOU WERE GOING TO LEAVE ME BEHIND!
MY BEST SCAVENGER? THAT WOULD BE BAD FOR BUSINESS.
THEY'RE GETTING AWAY! *BLAST THEM!*
SORRY ABOUT THIS.
WHA—?
THE HEAD!
THWAK
I'VE GOT IT BOSS!
THEN LET'S GET OUT OF HERE...

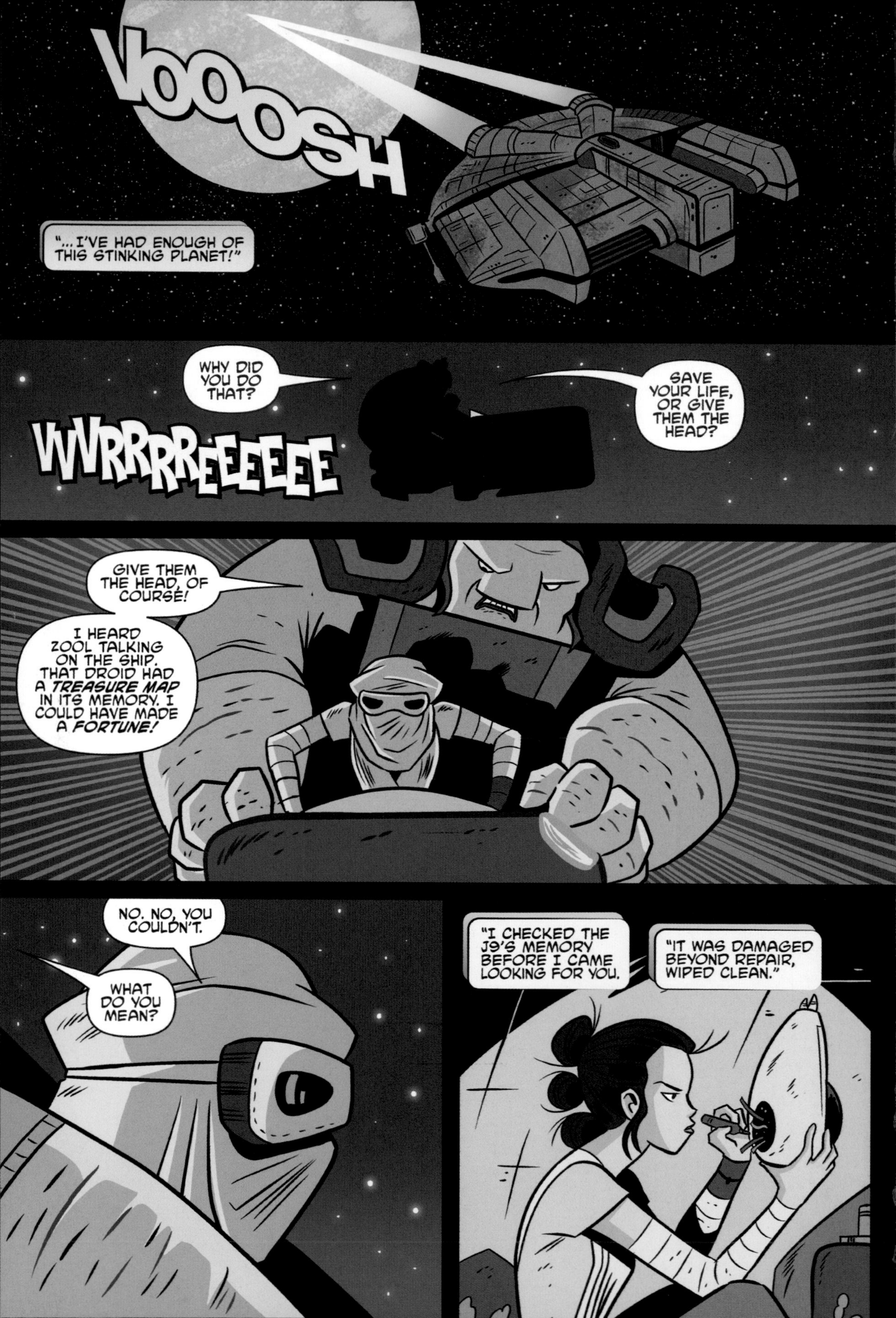
VOOOSH
"...I'VE HAD ENOUGH OF THIS STINKING PLANET!"
WHY DID YOU DO THAT?
VVVRRRREEEEEE
SAVE YOUR LIFE, OR GIVE THEM THE HEAD?
GIVE THEM THE HEAD, OF COURSE!
I HEARD ZOOL TALKING ON THE SHIP. THAT DROID HAD A *TREASURE MAP* IN ITS MEMORY. I COULD HAVE MADE A *FORTUNE!*
NO. NO, YOU COULDN'T.
WHAT DO YOU MEAN?
"I CHECKED THE J9'S MEMORY BEFORE I CAME LOOKING FOR YOU.
"IT WAS DAMAGED BEYOND REPAIR, WIPED CLEAN."

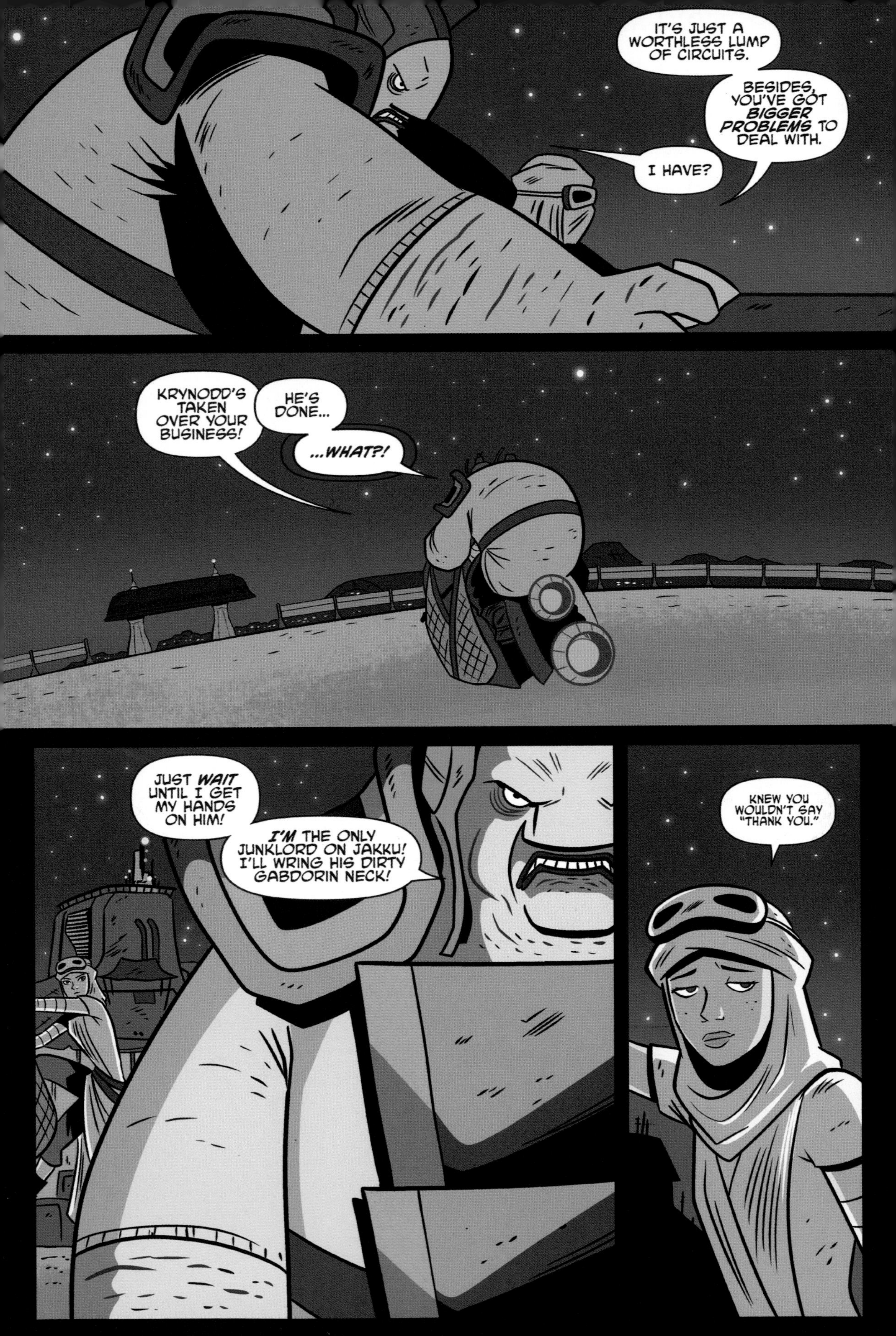
IT'S JUST A WORTHLESS LUMP OF CIRCUITS.
BESIDES, YOU'VE GOT BIGGER PROBLEMS TO DEAL WITH.
I HAVE?
KRYNODD'S TAKEN OVER YOUR BUSINESS!
HE'S DONE...
...WHAT?!
JUST WAIT UNTIL I GET MY HANDS ON HIM!
I'M THE ONLY JUNKLORD ON JAKKU! I'LL WRING HIS DIRTY GABDORIN NECK!
KNEW YOU WOULDN'T SAY "THANK YOU."

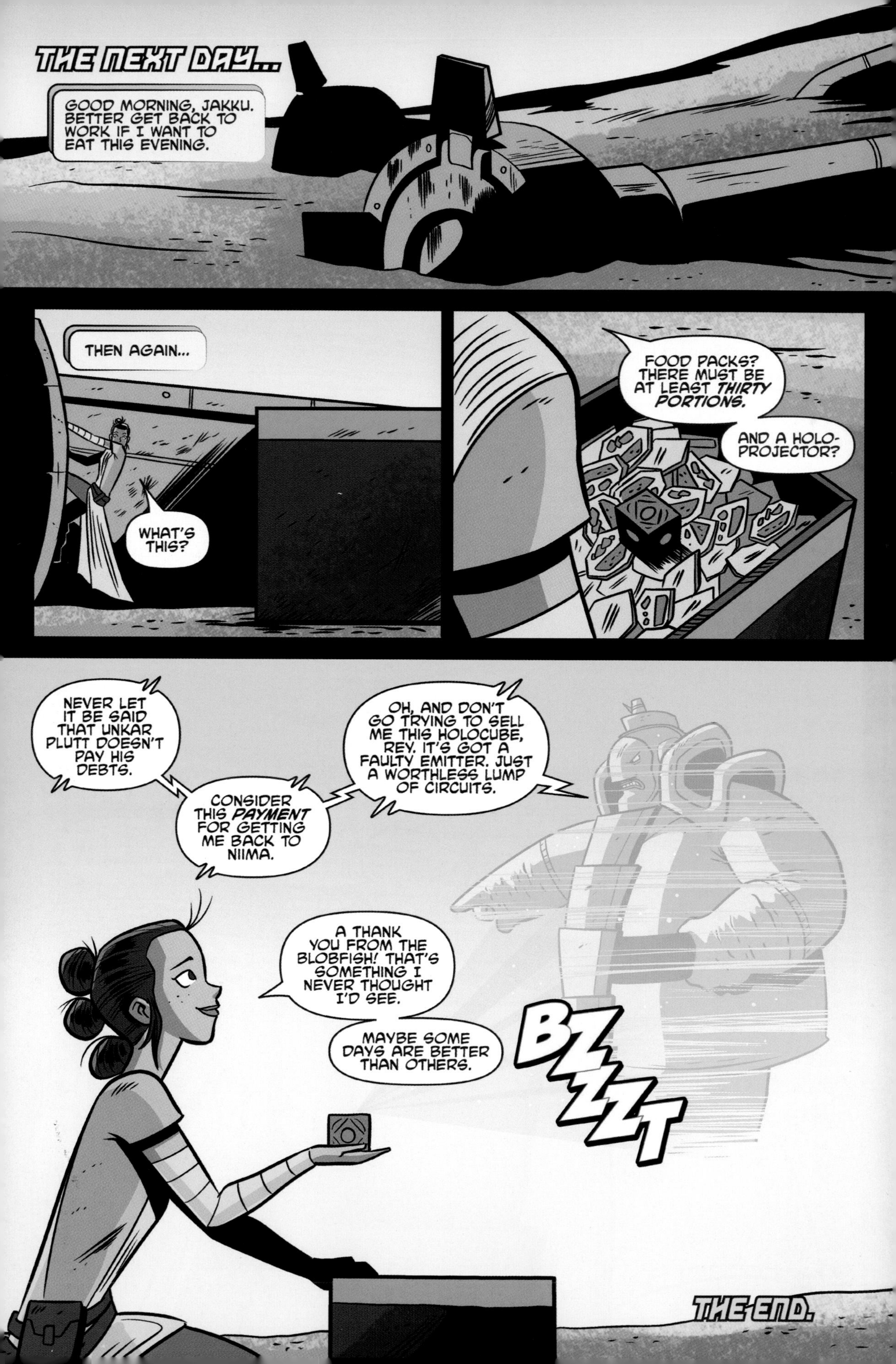
THE NEXT DAY...
GOOD MORNING, JAKKU. BETTER GET BACK TO WORK IF I WANT TO EAT THIS EVENING.
THEN AGAIN...
WHAT'S THIS?
FOOD PACKS? THERE MUST BE AT LEAST THIRTY PORTIONS.
AND A HOLO-PROJECTOR?
NEVER LET IT BE SAID THAT UNKAR PLUTT DOESN'T PAY HIS DEBTS.
CONSIDER THIS PAYMENT FOR GETTING ME BACK TO NIIMA.
OH, AND DON'T GO TRYING TO SELL ME THIS HOLOCUBE, REY. IT'S GOT A FAULTY EMITTER. JUST A WORTHLESS LUMP OF CIRCUITS.
A THANK YOU FROM THE BLOBFISH! THAT'S SOMETHING I NEVER THOUGHT I'D SEE.
MAYBE SOME DAYS ARE BETTER THAN OTHERS.
BZZZT
THE END.

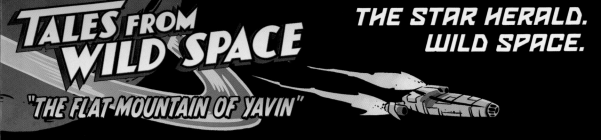

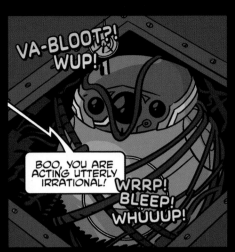

TALES FROM WILD SPACE
"THE FLAT MOUNTAIN OF YAVIN"
THE STAR HERALD. WILD SPACE.
VA-BLOOT?! WUP!
BOO, YOU ARE ACTING UTTERLY IRRATIONAL!
WRRP! BLEEP! WHUUUP!
NONSENSE! THE HYPER-DRIVE GENERATOR SURELY IS NOT TO BLAME FOR THIS MECHANICAL FAILURE! THE FUEL CELL MUST BE.
WHAT SEEMS TO BE THE PROBLEM, CRATER?
BOO BEING BOO, MASTER EMIL.
WHUUUP!
YOU WATCH YOUR LANGUAGE, STUBBORN SCRAP PILE!
HE REFUSES TO UNDERSTAND THAT THIS MAJOR MAL-FUNCTION WON'T BE SOLVED WITH SUCH A SMALL SOLUTION!
WHAT IF IT COULD, CRATER?
PLEASE, MASTER, ENLIGHTEN ME.
HAVE YOU EVER HEARD OF THE FLAT MOUNTAIN OF YAVIN?
I DON'T BELIEVE I HAVE, SIR.
"IT BEGINS IN THE DAYS FOLLOWING ONE OF THE FIRST REBEL ALLIANCE VICTORIES OVER THE EMPIRE.
"REBELS WERE HAPPILY CELEBRATING.
"BUT THE RESPITE WOULD BE SHORT-LIVED, AS THE MENACE ALREADY LOOMED."

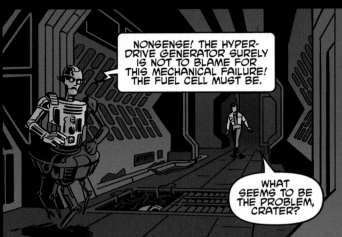

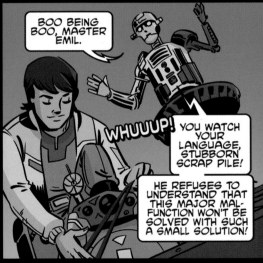

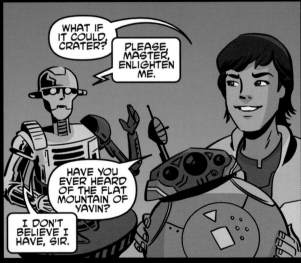

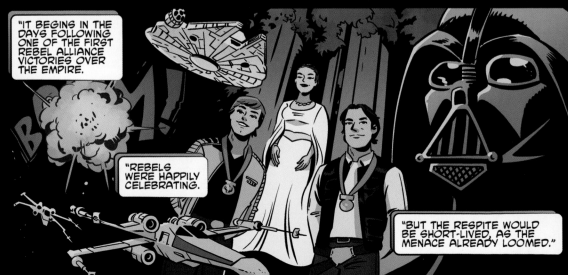

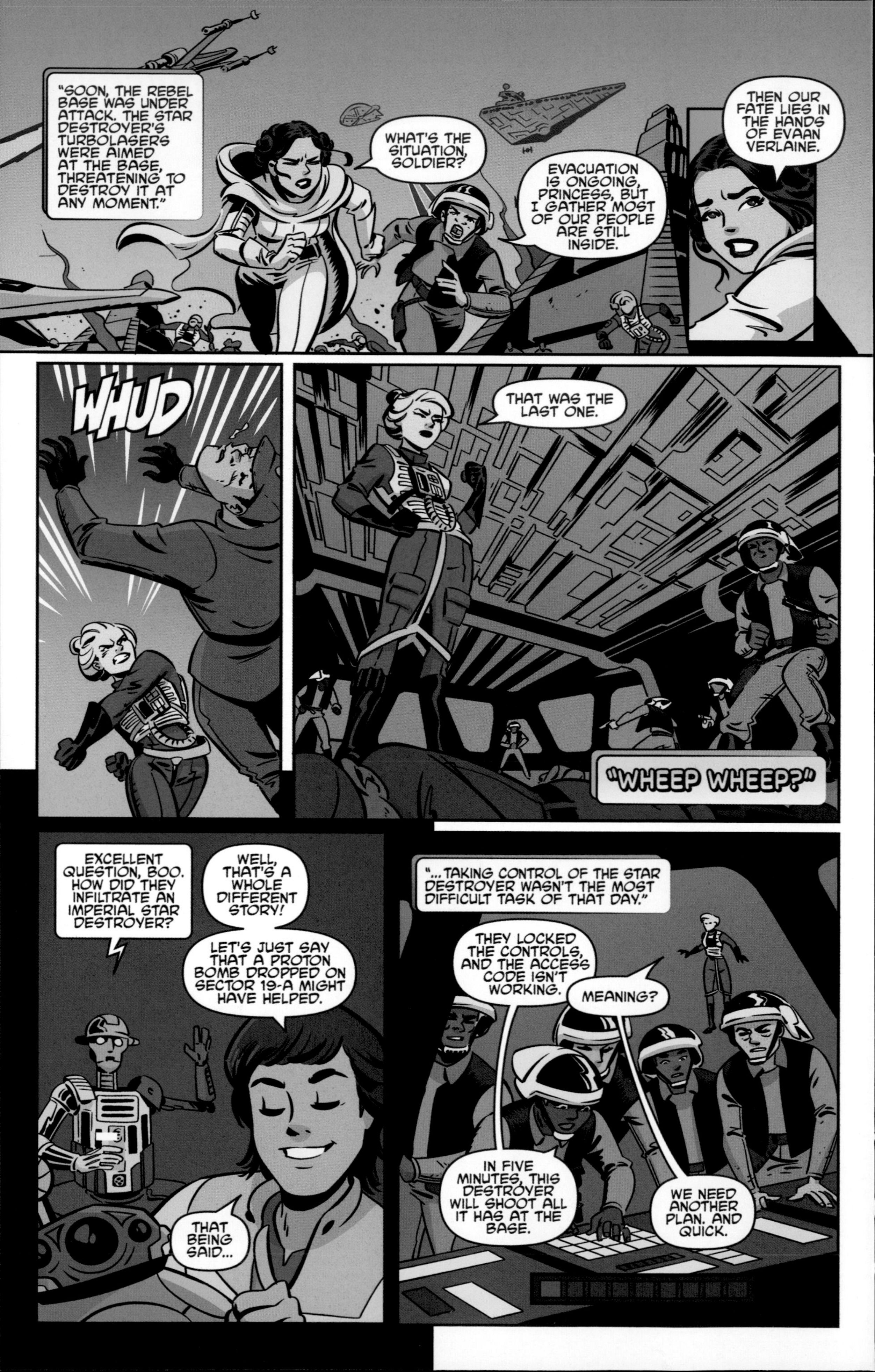
"SOON, THE REBEL BASE WAS UNDER ATTACK. THE STAR DESTROYER'S TURBOLASERS WERE AIMED AT THE BASE, THREATENING TO DESTROY IT AT ANY MOMENT."
WHAT'S THE SITUATION, SOLDIER?
EVACUATION IS ONGOING, PRINCESS, BUT I GATHER MOST OF OUR PEOPLE ARE STILL INSIDE.
THEN OUR FATE LIES IN THE HANDS OF EVAAN VERLAINE.
WHUD
THAT WAS THE LAST ONE.
"WHEEP WHEEP?"
EXCELLENT QUESTION, BOO. HOW DID THEY INFILTRATE AN IMPERIAL STAR DESTROYER?
WELL, THAT'S A WHOLE DIFFERENT STORY!
LET'S JUST SAY THAT A PROTON BOMB DROPPED ON SECTOR 19-A MIGHT HAVE HELPED.
THAT BEING SAID...
"...TAKING CONTROL OF THE STAR DESTROYER WASN'T THE MOST DIFFICULT TASK OF THAT DAY."
THEY LOCKED THE CONTROLS, AND THE ACCESS CODE ISN'T WORKING.
MEANING?
IN FIVE MINUTES, THIS DESTROYER WILL SHOOT ALL IT HAS AT THE BASE.
WE NEED ANOTHER PLAN. AND QUICK.

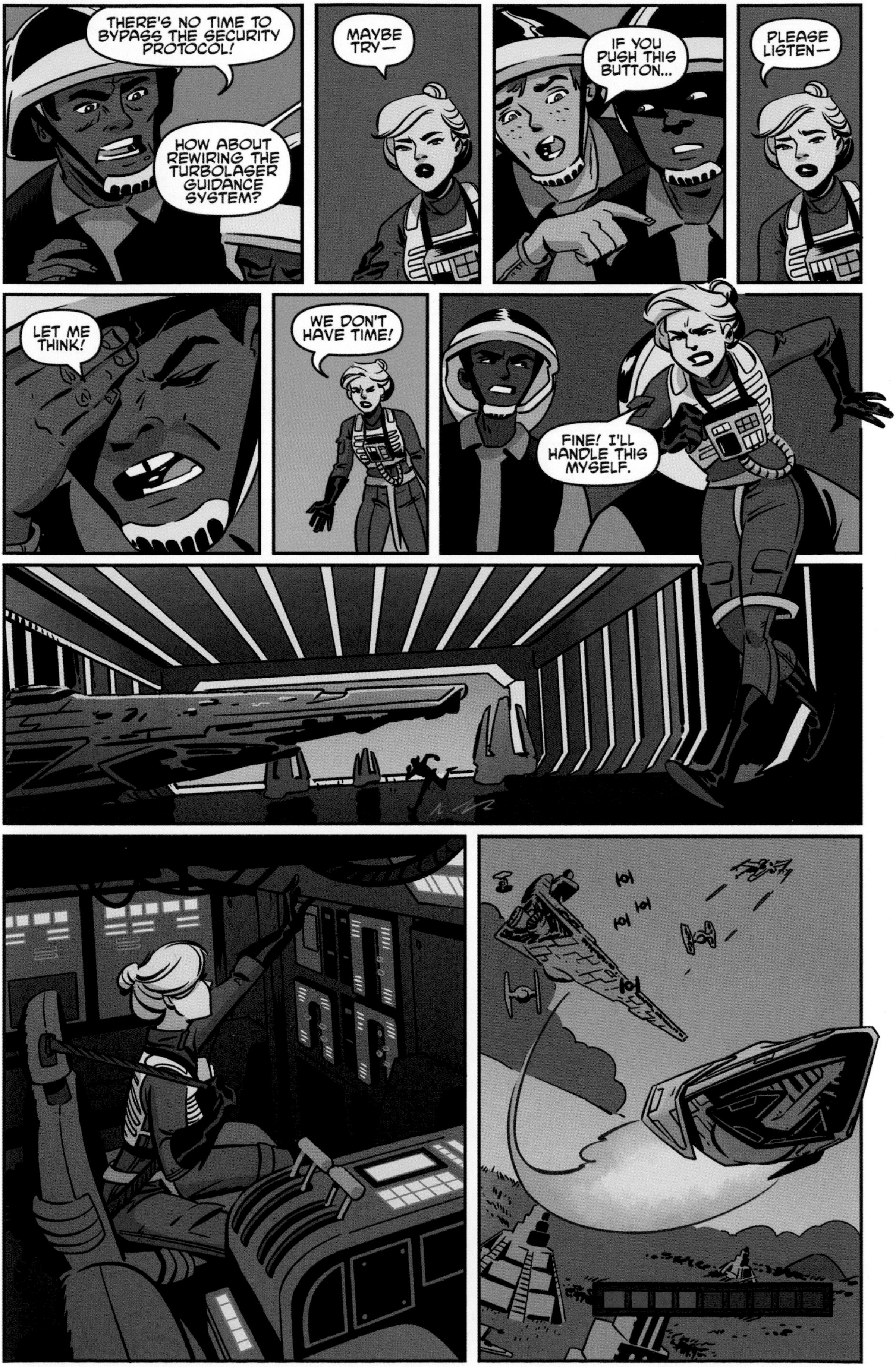
THERE'S NO TIME TO BYPASS THE SECURITY PROTOCOL!
HOW ABOUT REWIRING THE TURBOLASER GUIDANCE SYSTEM?
MAYBE TRY—
IF YOU PUSH THIS BUTTON...
PLEASE LISTEN—
LET ME THINK!
WE DON'T HAVE TIME!
FINE! I'LL HANDLE THIS MYSELF.

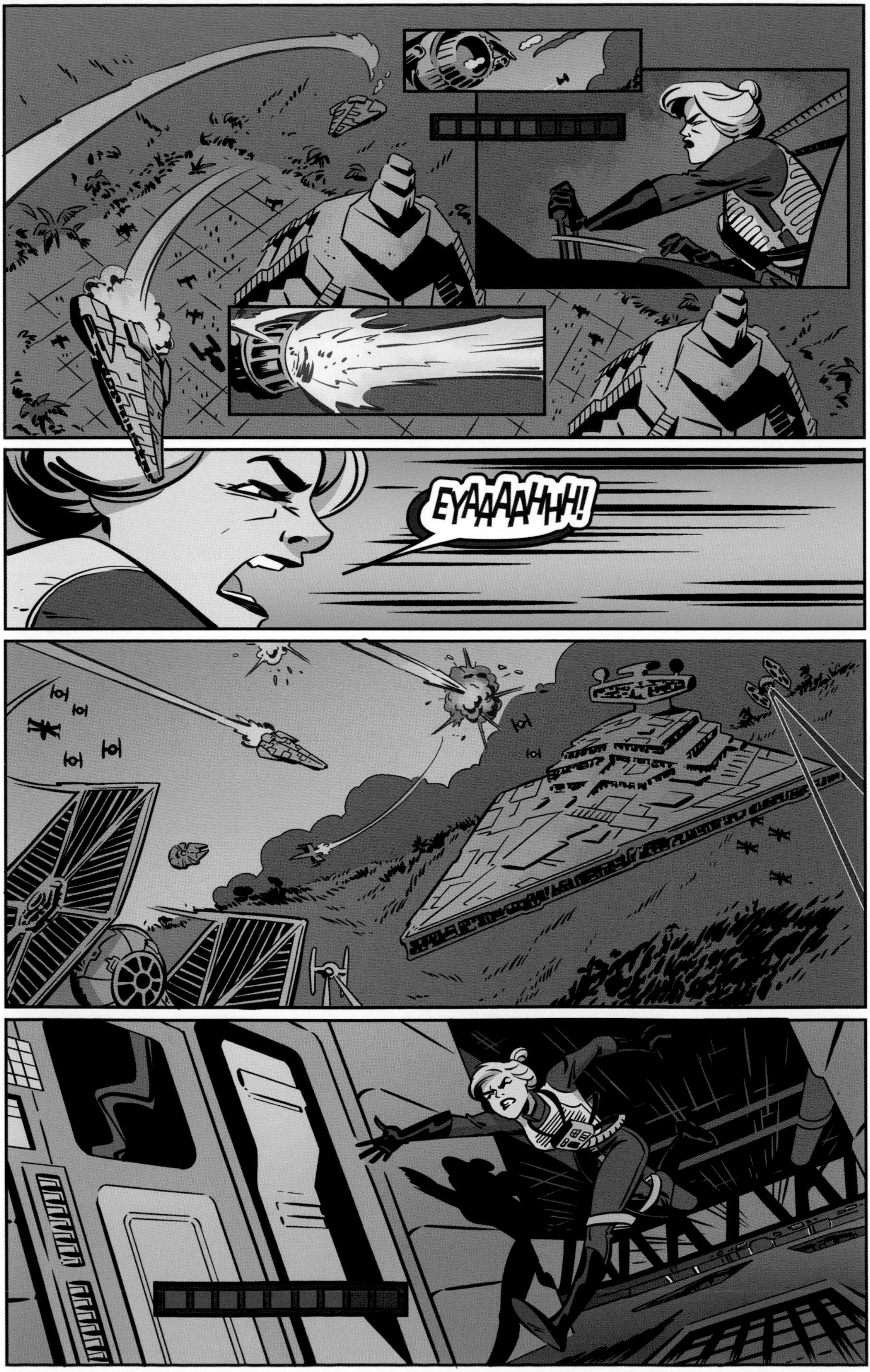
EYAAAAHHH!

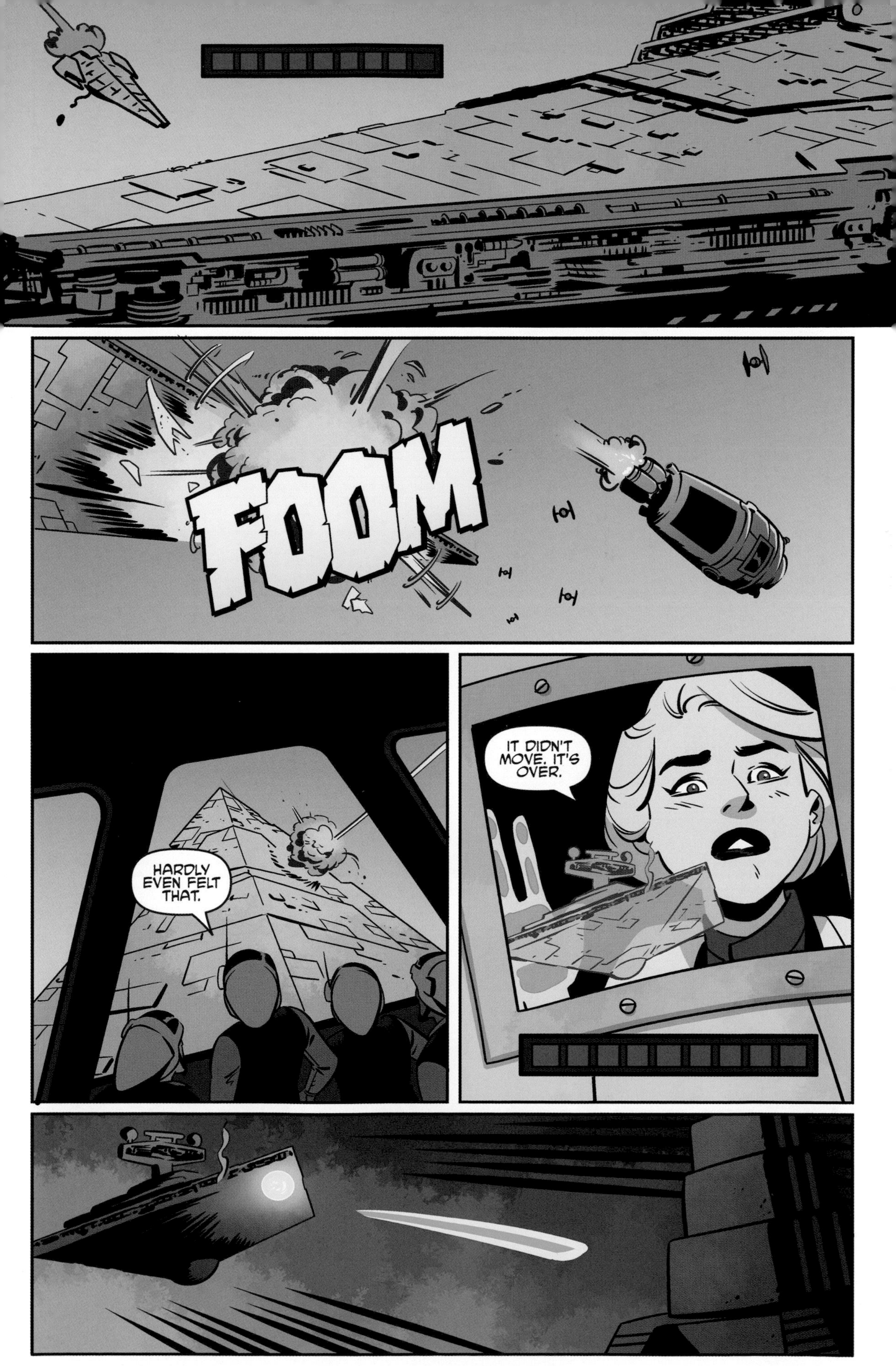
FOOM
HARDLY EVEN FELT THAT.
IT DIDN'T MOVE. IT'S OVER.

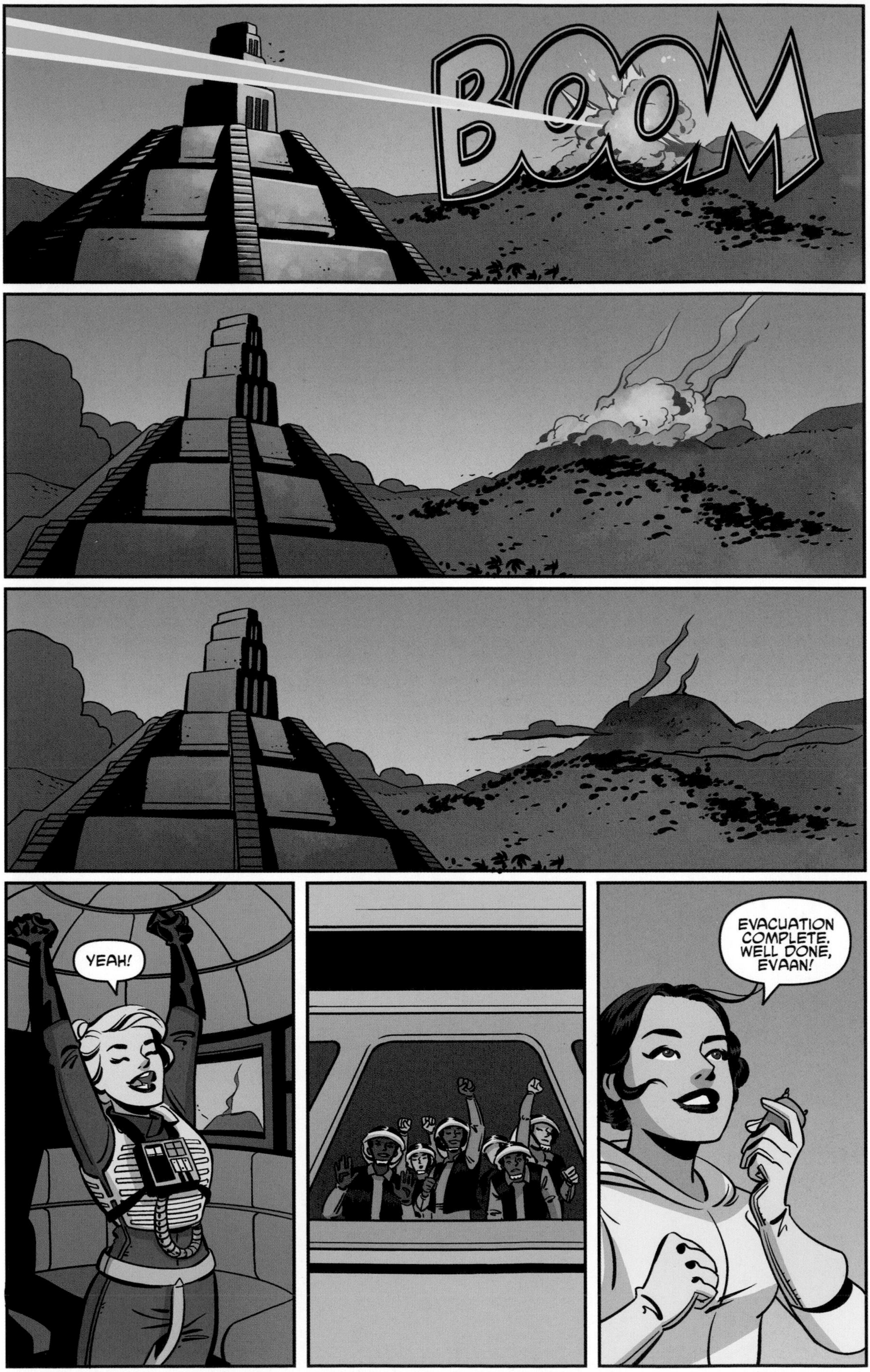
BOOM
YEAH!
EVACUATION COMPLETE. WELL DONE, EVAAN!

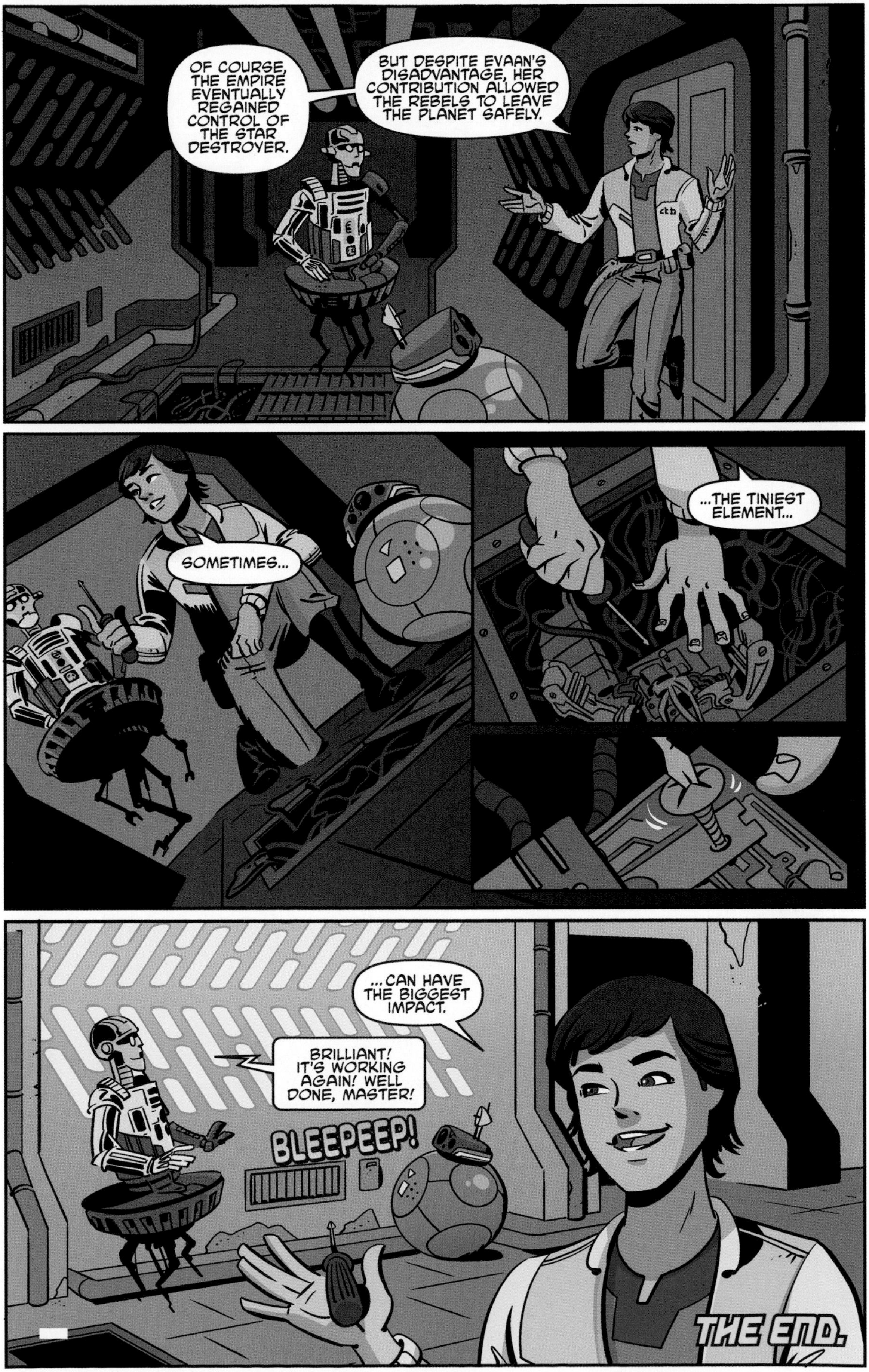
OF COURSE, THE EMPIRE EVENTUALLY REGAINED CONTROL OF THE STAR DESTROYER.
BUT DESPITE EVAAN'S DISADVANTAGE, HER CONTRIBUTION ALLOWED THE REBELS TO LEAVE THE PLANET SAFELY.
SOMETIMES...
...THE TINIEST ELEMENT...
...CAN HAVE THE BIGGEST IMPACT.
BRILLIANT! IT'S WORKING AGAIN! WELL DONE, MASTER!
BLEEPEEP!
THE END.

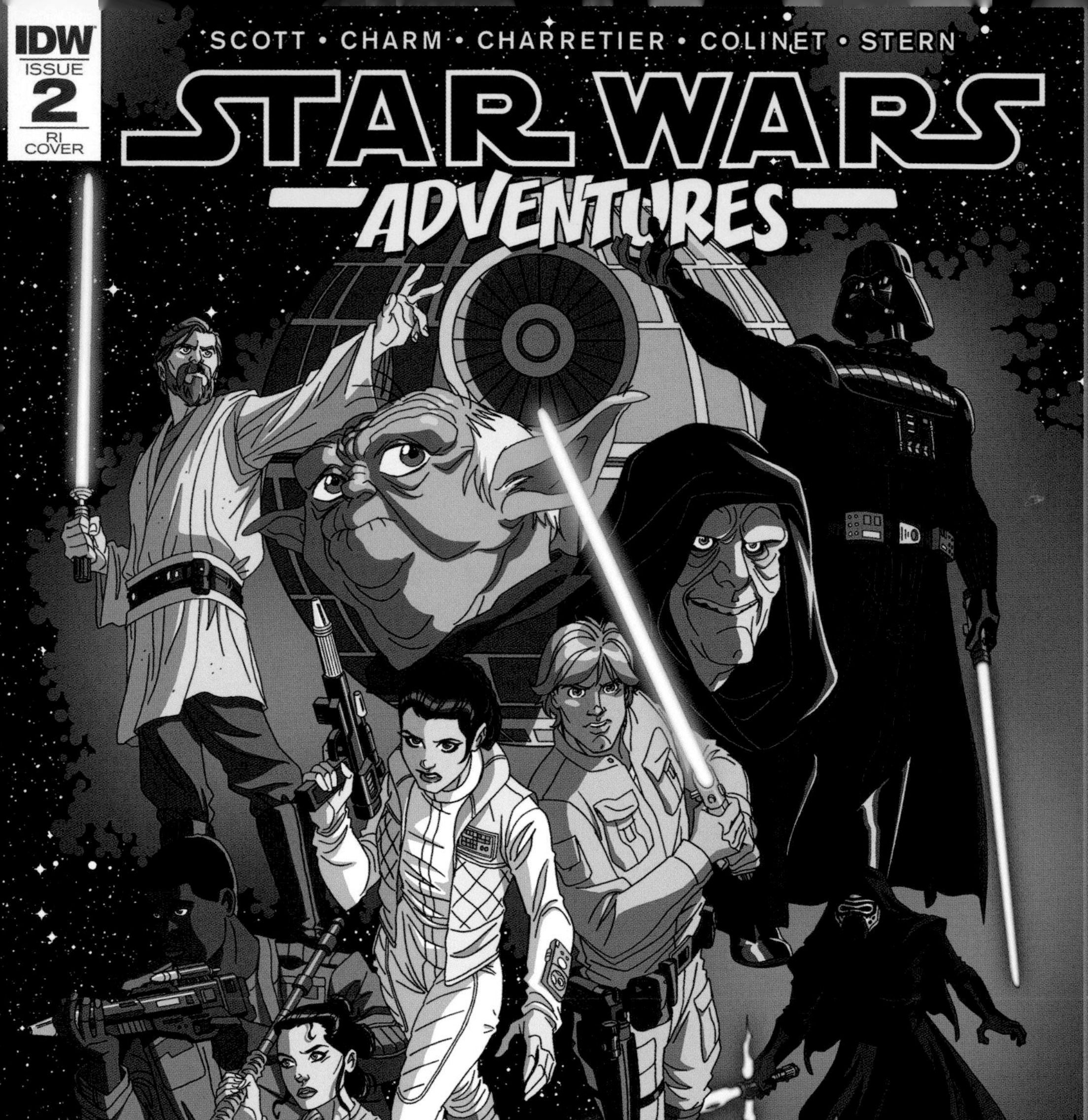
IDW
ISSUE
2
RI
COVER
SCOTT • CHARM • CHARRETIER • COLINET • STERN
STAR WARS
ADVENTURES

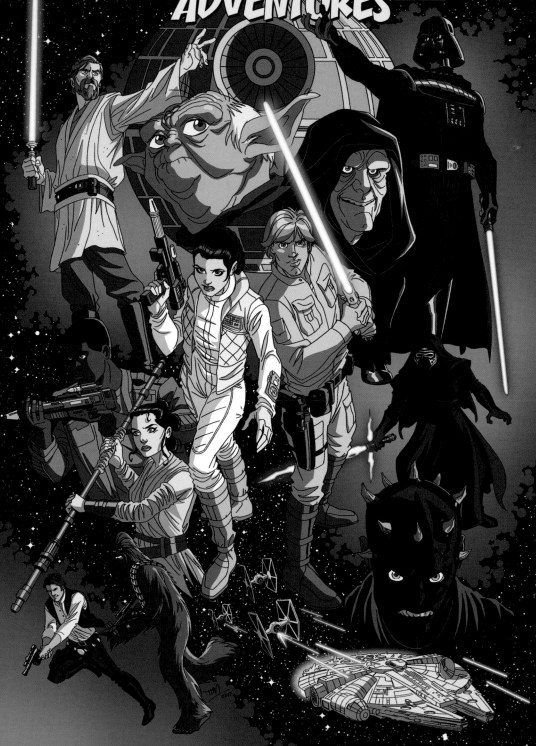

Star Wars Adventures #2
Variant cover RI artwork by Tim Levins